Erotic Stories for Women

Dirty Sex

Vivienne Dupont

Table of Contents

Table of Contents 3

A journey to the Mediterranean...5

A dominant Tinder date... 21

A special massage... 36

Turning 30 in a hostel in Barcelona 51

The Yoga Weekend 67

A journey to the Mediterranean

Finally, the annoying project that has been keeping me busy for months is finished. Angry customers, overstrained colleagues and dissatisfied bosses have been calling me constantly.

But now it's finally over. The project is off the table and I've taken two weeks off to celebrate!

Two weeks just for me. No cell phone. No laptop. No clients or colleagues.

I can't wait to do nothing all day.

And, in order to really enjoy my free time and make sure I don't get the idea to go into the office, I've decided to book a trip.

It was quite spontaneous in the travel agent as I didn't care about the destination, my only criteria was a 5-star hotel all-inclusive by the sea.

The nice lady was the first to suggest Spain to me. Mallorca. But it wasn't really tempting me. I don't want to lie by the pool hearing my neighbors next to me and anything work related they might be talking about.

So she kept searching and recommended Mykonos to me.

Mykonos... I know countless friends and colleagues who rave about their trip to Mykonos. I was actually thinking of something smaller and more discreet, but what are the chances I'd run into anyone I know there? Besides, the offer was unbeatable and the pictures she showed me are already getting me excited.

So Mykonos it was! I booked, paid and immediately received all travel documents.

I have never decided on anything quite so quickly.

I walked home afterwards with an excited spring in my step and the first thing I did was get my suitcase out. Even though it's cold and rainy here, a bright blue sky and 30 degrees await me in Mykonos, so it's time to pull out my skimpy bikinis and white crochet dresses and stow them in my suitcase.

I ask a friendly neighbor to look after my plants and take care of my letters for the next two weeks, and I head to bed early.

I'm full of anticipation and can't wait for the moment when I'm sitting by the pool in my unworn white bikini and sipping on my first cocktail.

And then finally the time has come. I take a cab to the airport, check in without any complications and land in Greece on time.

At the airport one of the tour operators is already standing to take me to the hotel, and before I know it, I arrive.

I can hardly believe my eyes. This one is definitely more beautiful than all the glossy pictures in the magazine, Instagram or anywhere else. The sea is incredibly blue and glistens in the sunlight. The houses are bright white and flowers are blooming everywhere. I take a deep breath and sigh out at the sights around me.

I get out of the car and watch the driver take my suitcases to the reception.

I take one last look around before I follow him and then check in.

Everyone is incredibly nice and I'm shown everything on the way to my room, including the dining area, the pool, the access to the beach.

I'm speechless, which is pretty unheard of for me. I feel overwhelmed with satisfaction - Who would have expected that a last minute vacation could be such a hit?

The hotel concierge opens my room door and puts the card into the slot provided so that the light comes on. But I don't need that at this time of day, because the large windows flood the room with light.

Still speechless, I slip inside what will be my home for the next two weeks. I have rarely seen anything so beautiful. The walls are very high and everywhere are hanging pictures of regional artists. It's not just a standard hotel room, but almost a small apartment. I have a bedroom, a huge bathroom and a living room with a cosy sitting area as well as a balcony with an infinity pool.

I give the bellman a little tip and then close the door behind me. I wouldn't have expected this even in my dreams.

I walk up to the balcony and can look out over the blue, glistening sea while relaxing in my own pool.

Wow.

I sit down on the comfortable lounge furniture to get my bearings.

Then I look at the note that the receptionist gave me and on which I can find information about the all-inclusive offer.

I look at the clock. Lunch is already over, but I can get snacks and cocktails at the large hotel pool and decide that I might as well start the holiday as I mean to go on and take advantage of the offer.

I quickly unpack my suitcase and slip into my new bikini and a white dress, which has never had the opportunity to be shown off before!

Then I slide on my new best sandals and go on an exploration tour.

The hotel is more of a complex. There's no big main building, where there are simply hotel rooms next to hotel rooms, but several small buildings that house a few rooms and apartments. This of course makes the whole complex very spacious, but there are countless quiet places where you can retreat.

I find the pool and sit down at one of the white tables and immediately an attentive employee approaches me and hands me the card.

I decide on some finger food and a white wine to start with.

He brings me everything and then stops at my table to ask if I have any more wishes. I deny. But he still won't leave. He wants to know if I am here all alone. I nod and can see that pity is in his eyes. He's probably thinking 'Such a beautiful woman. All alone. How sad.'

I find him a bit pushy and explain that my fiancé has given me a vacation all to myself because I took over the wedding planning all by myself. Of course this is not true, but it's good for him to think that I'm in steady hands.

He nods understandingly and disappears again.

Then I take the time to have a look around. The hotel is pretty busy and according to the travel agency employee, it's always fully booked during the peak season because it's so popular, especially with couples. I look around and see this to be true, and most of them my age, around early 30's.

Occasionally I see smaller groups of friends and even a few people travelling alone.

At least they don't *look* like they're waiting for anyone else.

But I don't want to think about the other guests. With my own pool I'll only have to have human contact when my stomach growls. And even then, I can have everything brought to my room. What a delight!

I eat up and then go to my balcony until dinner.

The weather is wonderful. There is a refreshing wind, but not so strong that it would mess up my hair or blow away my towel.

Everything is really perfect as it is.

I spend the first days sunbathing, swimming and eating. I can really feel my muscles relaxing and my head finally coming down again. But then, I begin to get bored. I've already finished my books, even watched all episodes of my favorite series that have been left behind in the last months.

I have a desire for exercise and to move my body. At home I do yoga, go boxing and run my 10 km round every morning.

Here I swim every day, but it's not enough for me in the long run.

I watch the sports program to see what's on. Boxing and yoga are also available here, but I'm in the mood for some variety. Tennis for example. If that's already offered, why not?

I go to the reception and ask if it would be possible to get me in a course at short notice, but the lady behind the counter shakes her head.

"All beginner courses are full," she says regretfully.

"Oh. I'm not a beginner anymore. I played when I was young. That was 15 years ago, but I certainly still master the basic things today."

"Oh, well, in that case, we have a few trainers who offer private lessons. I can see if anyone has time for you."

"Wonderful", I say with satisfaction and write down my room number for her.

No sooner am I back in my room than the phone rings and the same lady I was talking to a moment ago announces that I can take my first tennis lesson tonight.

Exuberantly I agree, but then comes the great realization: I didn't pack any things that are suitable for tennis.

There would be my top and my leggings, which I always use for yoga, but they're not really ideal for tennis. And neither are my sports shoes.

I think about whether I should go and buy something quickly, but then I find that I'm questioning myself. Who knows how often I'll even play tennis? Once or twice? It's really not worth it.

So I decide to stick with my tight yoga pants and the t-shirt and lace up my running shoes.

I arrive at the tennis court and stand around a little lost. I don't even know the name of my coach. Or whether it's a woman or a man. Suddenly I feel really stupid. What kind of idea was this?

"Hello! Are you Jana", I hear a male voice asking. I turn around and look at the most beautiful man I've ever seen. Oh my God. He looks like a Greek god. He's about 1.90 m tall, has broad shoulders, a well-trained upper body and dark brown, almost black hair, which he keeps combing back with his hands so that it doesn't fall on his face. Plus the greenest eyes I have ever seen. His tan is perfectly accentuated by his bright white tennis outfit and I suddenly feel like I'm 14 again, facing my crush from a step above me.

"Yes. I am Jana," I say after what feels like an eternity. He looks at me confused. Yes, I know. These aren't tennis clothes. But I don't have anything else and suddenly I feel totally stupid. Maybe this really wasn't the best idea.

"Was tennis a spontaneous idea of yours?" he asks me.

"Yes... I thought I was just doing yoga here on the beach, but then I got carried away with the urge to exercise."

"Well, that'll be fine. Come on, let's find you a bat first. I'm Nikos, by the way."

Nikos. What a fitting name for such an image of a man.

He leads me into a small equipment room and hands me a racket that suits me well.

And then it starts. Nikos is a very good coach, praises me when I do something right, gives constructive criticism when I'm bad. I feel as if I never stopped training and learning the whole lesson.

"You're really good," he praised me as we stood on the square afterwards, snorting.

"Thank you," I reply breathlessly. He really challenged me.

"How long are you here for?"

I quickly do the math.

"Eight days left."

"Then we can train at least four more times."

"Okay!" I say euphorically. More because I'm happy to be able to watch him for an hour and less because I want to continue training.

I quickly run back to my room, take a long shower and then go out for some food. Today I want to try the beach bar for the first time. My usual evening routine
14

has become going to my balcony with a bottle of wine and watching the sunset from there. But today I feel like a change, so live music and cocktails it is!

I put on one of my pretty white dresses and then settle down at one of the small tables. Again as I look around, I notice everyone is here at least in pairs or in groups and I can already feel the pitying looks of the others because I'm sitting here all alone. But I don't mind. I enjoy the music, the view of the sea and my delicious cocktail.

"Darling, won't you join us?", I suddenly hear the voice of an elderly lady say. She stands in front of me and points to a table with other ladies her age.

"No, thanks. I really enjoy being alone right now," I reply with a smile.

"Oh. You're just thinking that. Socialising would be much better."

"No, no. I come from the big city. Every minute without people is precious to me," I now say somewhat more directly. She looks at me without understanding, but then leaves again.

Relieved, I take a deep breath and roll my eyes to myself. You go on vacation alone and still you aren't left alone.

"The ladies only meant it nicely", I suddenly hear someone else say again. I just want to turn around annoyed and give him a nasty saying, because I think it's the pushy waiter from last time, but suddenly Nikos is standing in front of my table.

"Oh", is the only thing that comes out.

"They do this to every woman travelling alone," he continues.

"That's very nice. But I just don't want to."

"Why not? You don't seem like an unsociable person."

"I'm not. But I'm on vacation. I don't want to have to talk to people I'm not really interested in anyway. And what could I talk about with the old ladies? I prefer to enjoy my time here alone," I answer honestly.

"I see. And company of people you could talk to? About tennis, for example."

Confused I look at him. Does he mean himself?

"They would be okay," I say cautiously and see a broad smile spread across his face. He sits down on the free chair opposite me and orders a glass of wine.

"You don't mind, do you?"

How could I!

We start to talk. About the island, the hotel complex, tennis and later also about personal matters. I find out that he recently broke up with his girlfriend and is now looking for distance here.

It gets later and later and at some point we're the last ones at the beach bar. We finish our drinks and Nikos suggests that we could go for a walk on the beach. He has his first lesson in the afternoon.

I agree of course. How could I not? He's such a beautiful man and his company is very pleasant. Besides, I can guess what this is going to amount to and I'm absolutely ready for it. A nice adventure with a beautiful Greek man on the beach would be the icing on the cake to my already perfect trip.

We land in a small quiet bay. Of course there isn't a soul to be seen and we are among ourselves.

He suggests that we sit in the sand and I agree. His arm naturally wraps around my shoulder and he pulls me towards him. And then it happens naturally. He kisses me.

It's one of those magical kisses. Very gentle and careful, but soon it turns into passionate kissing that turns into a fumbling. His big hands are on my breasts, on my hips, on my legs. I feel them everywhere. I feel his breath getting heavier and his lust increasing.

He pulls the dress over my head and kisses my naked skin.

Soon I'm lying in the sand and he's above me. He pulls his t-shirt over his head and his perfect upper body is gently illuminated by the moonlight. It's simply unbelievable how good he looks.

I run over his smooth skin with my fingertips, tracing his muscles until at some point I reach his crotch. He stands up again briefly, takes off his pants and then kneels next to me so that I can work his cock with my hand. And how could it be any different. He is big, thick and perfect. I can hardly wait to finally feel him inside me.

Meanwhile his hand moves between my legs. He pushes my slip aside and strokes carefully through my cleft before he devotes himself to my clitoris.

Very slowly, he passes his fingertip over it, stroking and teasing it again and again until I close my eyes and moan softly. It feels *so* good.

Then he moves. His tail slides out of my hand and he now kneels between my legs. Carefully he pulls my panties off my hips and then bends down deeply with his face. Again I feel a slight tickle on my pearl. It is

18

his tongue. He licks me now. First very gently, then a little stronger and more intense. My hands claw into the sand and I feel my abdomen tightening more and more. If he continues like this, I'll be right there.

Then I feel his fingers glide across my wet hole. First he plays with it and then he slowly penetrates me with one finger. Once inside, he turns it and bends it so that it presses exactly against my most sensitive spot. And with that he has me. I groan and push my pelvis towards him a little more. He keeps licking, keeps pressing his finger on that one spot and then as the pressure builds more and more, I come, powerfully and loudly.

He lets me take a deep breath once before he withdraws from me. He seeks my gaze and smiles at me as I look at him as well.

Then he spreads my legs again, bends over me with his upper body and puts his cock on my sensitive pussy. I groan loudly as I feel him penetrate me. Oh my god. He is so big and hard and fills me up perfectly. I can feel him slowly squeezing in and out. He puts his arms down next to my head, he's watching me very closely as he gets faster.

My arms now clasp his upper body and my legs lie on his back. I feel him now deep inside me. And I also feel the next climax coming up inside me. He is getting even faster, even harder and then I come another time.

Oh wow. My whole body begins to tremble and finds no end. Everything twitches and trembles with excitement.

I hear how he too moans louder, breathes more intensely and then I feel his twitching within me. He also comes and injects his complete charge into me. This makes me extremely horny and I get even wetter and still feel everything in my body in motion.

He puts his upper body on mine, takes one deep breath and I can feel how fast his heart is beating.

Very carefully and slowly he withdraws from me again and his face beams towards me.

He gives me a tender kiss before we wordlessly get dressed again and head back to the hotel complex.

We say goodbye in front of my room.

"See you at practice?" he asks hesitantly.

"Absolutely", I reply and look forward to it now.

A dominant Tinder date

Another weekend alone on the sofa. All my friends are now in relationships and doing something with their partners, visiting their family or having fun with their siblings' children. All this adult stuff I have no desire for, at least not for a very long time.

I start watching a series, but somehow it doesn't grab me. I can't give her the attention she probably deserves. Instead, I pick up my cell phone, scroll through my timeline for what might be the hundredth time that day to see if there is anything new. But there's nothing.

"What are you doing?", I ask my best friend in the hope that she will have some time for me after all.

"We're on our way to my parents' house right now."

We...by that she means her boyfriend and herself. Urgh...

I put the cell phone away again and make myself a bowl of popcorn. I have a theory that I can follow the series better with it, but it doesn't seem to work.

I pick up my cell phone again and go through the apps. Mhh... Tinder. I haven't looked there for days. Maybe something new has come up there.

I open it up and I can see directly that I have a few new matches, and some even wrote me. The message sounds really interesting, at least in my current situation, so bored and alone sitting on the sofa.

"Hello Lara. My name is Jens and I like your pictures. Imagine me ringing at your front door tonight. You open the door for me. Lightly dressed and already have your favorite toy ready in the bedroom so we can use it right away.

You don't say a word, but simply invite me in with a gesture of your hand or close the door again immediately if you don't like me in real life.

I brought handcuffs and a blindfold. We can use both if you agree.

You invite me in, and while doing so, you undress and drop your clothes on the floor in the hallway. Before you enter the bedroom, you're already naked. I put the handcuffs on you and tie you to the bed. Then comes the blindfold, and the game begins..."

First I laugh and think to myself 'what kind of shit is this?' But then I look at his pictures. He looks very good already. Tall, trained, dark hair, nice face.

22

What's wrong with a little fun? I mean, I have nothing else to do anyway.

I answer him. At first rather jokingly. I do not want to go into his suggestion. Who would be prepared to be tied up by a complete stranger? I'm not insane.

But then the conversation develops and somehow there is something about him that doesn't let me press the "de-match" button directly.

After all, you don't experience something like this every day. That is, that a complete stranger, attractive man wants to come home to you, blindfold you, tie you to the bed and then do what he wants with you. And what I want. That's what we're writing about right now. He knows my preferences and knows that I prefer to be licked to the climax while his fingers stimulate me from the inside.

He promises that I will experience the most powerful orgasm of my life and I wonder how he can prove it. He does not know me at all. How can he give me such a great orgasm?

Another message pops up and contains his cell phone number. He wants to hear my voice and convince me with his that we will do this tonight.

I dial his number. What do I have to lose?

Well, and then ... yes, then I somehow accepted. His voice almost drove me crazy. So deep, so masculine, so dominant. It only took him two minutes to convince me to come over.

And now I'm standing in my bedroom in front of the wardrobe and thinking about what to wear. There is no way I can keep my sweatpants on. It should be something beautiful. Not necessarily my most expensive lingerie with suspenders and hold-ups, but still tasteful.

I decide to wear a black lace set and put on a black silk robe. Not quite transparent, but transparent enough to guess what might be underneath.

Then I quickly tidy up my apartment, shave and quickly empty my glass of wine. I am already a little nervous.

"Are you ready?" I read on my phone.

"Yes", I answer quickly before I can change my mind again.

"Then I'm standing at the front door."

I feel my heart start beating faster and my hands start shaking. This is completely insane. What I am doing here?

I go to the intercom and can't move. I do not have to open the door. I can block his number now and then never hear from him again.

Then suddenly the doorbell rings and I flinch. I automatically press the door buzzer and hear the front door being pushed open at the bottom.

He comes into the house, runs up the stairs and then he stands in front of me.

Whew ... that's a beautiful man.

"Hey", he says and stops in front of me without moving. He waits for me to invite him in.

I remember that I have to be quiet and that is difficult for me. Really hard. When I am nervous, I talk like a waterfall.

I keep looking at him. Look at his beautiful face, down on his broad shoulders and a well-defined body. I'd be stupid to just send one of these guys away again.

So I invite him in and try to remember what happened next.

I am supposed to slowly undress in front of him as I head for my bedroom.

So I open the robe, strip it off my shoulder and then unbutton my bra. I save the panties for last while standing in the doorway to my bedroom.

I bend down, take them off quickly and then go into my dimly lit room.

I turn around and see how he looks at me with satisfaction. He has a blindfold in his hand and holds it up questioningly. I nod. Also to the handcuffs. Now nothing else matters. He comes closer to me and then puts the blindfold on me. I look once more into his beautiful face and then everything goes dark.

Every movement now becomes more intense. I feel his hot breath on my naked skin and smell his irresistible perfume, which he has put on. Then he turns me around and I feel a slight pressure on my shoulder. I am supposed to go first and he leads me directly to my bed, on which I am supposed to lie down.

His hands grab my wrists and pull them up.

I feel the cold metal on my skin and hear the rattling of the chain that connects the handcuffs.

Then I hear the click. My left hand is now in the handcuffs and is pulled to my metal bed frame, through which he now pulls the other handcuffs.

He takes my right hand and puts one of the metal shackles on as well and fastens me to the bed with it. I hear the click again. Now I'm stuck and can no longer move.

I feel my heart beating faster and my head slowly realizing that I am now at the mercy of this strange man.

Tense and nervous I stay lying down. I have no other choice anyway.

I flinch when I feel his hand on my body. He runs his fingertips over my naked skin. He starts with my shoulders, works his way down to my collarbones and then to my breasts. Gently he circles my nipples and waits until they get hard. I can feel his fingers on them, how he tugs and squeezes them and then a sharp pain runs through me. Clamps on my nipples. Phew... I grit my teeth and take a deep breath.

He asked me in our previous foreplay exchanges if I like that. I have never tried it before, but I wrote that I can imagine it. And now I have these two heavy clamps on my hard nipples and I don't know if I should find it horrible or really cool.

I try to bear the pain as he moves his fingers further down until he reaches my crotch. The pain turns into pure excitement and my nipples become even harder. With his fingers he moves over my opening and I hear a smacking sound. A smacking, because my pussy is already so wet.

Apparently, according to my moans and body pulsations, I am very pleased with all of this.

His fingers continue to wander, first circling around my clitoris, pressing them gently into my wet hole before he starts to fuck me with them.

Then, he pulls his fingers out again, places his hands on my thighs and pushes them far apart.

I hear him walking around the room, apparently looking for something. I assume my favourite toy. I was supposed to put that out, but in all the excitement I forgot. I quickly try to orientate myself and point to my bedside drawer next to me.

I hear him open it and rummage around in it a little. I quickly think about what I have put in there and I think everything I own is in there. Vibrators, dildos, plugs. In all possible sizes.

I hear him taking out the first part and then pressing the power button.

Phew... with that he immediately hit the most intense part, namely my *Magic Wand*, which switches on directly with the strongest level.

I flinch when I feel the strong vibration on my body. He drives it along my arms, over my stomach and then over my legs. He starts with my toes and works his way up until he reaches my crotch.

My heart is beating because I know he is going to press the part right on my clitoris and then it will only take seconds until I come.

I feel it on my outer labia, then on my inner labia and then on my hole. Then it goes a little bit deeper up to my ass and then higher again until it reaches my clitoris.

And then I flinch and ripple with intensity. He presses the vibrator firmly on my bead while my whole body is tense and awaiting the release. My legs are pressed far apart, my pelvis is lifting higher and higher, and then I come. Totally uncontrolled in my blissful letting go.

"Oh, that was fast," I hear him mumbling. He switches the vibrator off again and puts it aside. Fortunately. It would have driven me completely crazy if he would have held it to my totally overexcited clit for any longer.

I feel his hands touching my crotch again. He glides his fingers over my wet lips and taps with his finger on my bead. Yes. I still flinch when you touch it. I need a short breather. I really want to say something, but I really want to play the game and just let him do it. He will make sure that I don't lose my fun in it.

And indeed, he leaves those most sensitive parts alone. Instead, he now takes care of my opening. He has taken a big dildo out of my drawer and is now pushing it into me without warning. Again, I groan. My body rears up and I enjoy how this toy just fills me up. But what I especially enjoy is that it is being led by a man who is actually a complete stranger to me and yet has blindly tied me to my bed.

I feel that the climax hasn't quite subsided yet and I know that I really don't need much at this stage to come back again.

He fucks me with the dildo, bangs me hard again and again and as I predicted, I come another time.

I groan loudly, my body rebounds again and then I feel it slowly retreating. The dildo disappears from me and I hear how he is looking for something else. I hear a tube being opened. That must be my lubricant. I can guess what he pulled out of my drawer next. And indeed. I feel something cold, metallic on my butt. My plug.

I take a deep breath. Try to relax a little and let the climax fade away.

I can feel the tip of my narrow hole and how it pushes against it lightly, but also decisively.

I notice how it slowly penetrates me and then I breathe a sigh of relief when the thickest part has passed my muscle and it is inside me.

I hear the click from the tube, which he now puts aside again.

What happens now?

I hear him getting up again. He should be standing right next to me now. But he's not moving.

Then I suddenly feel a sharp pain. The clamps on my nipples. I have completely forgotten them. But now I remember them again because he moves them. He pulls on them. Sometimes a little bit lighter, then again a little bit stronger.

Phew. I want to protest, want to beat his hand off, but I can't move and I don't want to say anything because somehow it also feels extremely sexy.

Then a sharp, stabbing pain runs through me and suddenly it's all over. He takes the clamps off again, and I take another deep breath and then flinch because he touches my clitoris. His fingers run over my cleft, which is now soaking wet again.

He pushes my legs wide apart and then I feel a wiggle. He is sitting back down on the bed. He keeps spreading my legs and then I feel something tickling my thighs. His hair. He brings his very close to my pussy and then starts to lick me.

Phew... after the pain it feels really incredible how he licks very gently with his tongue through my cleft and then circles around my clitoris. Over and over again.

My pelvis presses itself against him again. And then he finally pushes two fingers into my wet hole. I feel him pressing against the plug with them and then moving them in the other direction. Right at my most sensitive point.

He fingers me and licks me and although my last orgasm was not long ago, I realize that the next one won't be long to arrive again.

Again and again he circles my clitoris with his tongue, presses his fingers against my G-spot and then it's done. My belly tenses up, my legs as well and then I come.

And how...

Again he retreats while I breathe in and out deeply to get clear again.
I hear the rustling of cloth now. Is he finally unpacking his cock?

32

He moves down from the bed again and I feel his hands on mine. He releases the bonds and pulls the mask from my eyes.

Is he finished already?

Questioningly I look at him. He goes back a little bit and then takes off his clothes very slowly. He opens his belt and his pants and lets them sink to the floor. His hard cock comes out, which is long and thick.

He does not say a word and just looks at me. Then he comes back on the bed and grabs me. First he turns me on my stomach and then pulls my pelvis up to him.

Yeah, he's fucking me now. God, it's all hot.

His hand moves over my ass, presses strongly on the plug once more so that I groan and then I feel a sharp pain on my right ass cheek, on which he has clapped his hand. And then the left one follows. Phew. I close my eyes, enjoy the pain racing through my body and then lay my head down on my crossed arms.

And then he finally penetrates me. And even though he has occupied himself with me for the last two hours and made me come again and again, it now somehow feels like a release. It feels so good to feel his cock inside me. Again and again he pulls it out completely and then pushes it back in completely. With every push he gets a little bit faster and harder.

His right hand keeps pressing or pulling on the plug.

Everything feels so intense and so good.

All of a sudden I hear a buzzing sound again and only a few seconds later I feel the Magic Wand on my clitoris again. Oh man. So I come right back.

He now pushes his cock with all his strength into my wet pussy, while the vibrator continues to press on my clit.

I'm coming. Fierce. My body is rippling, but he holds me down while he keeps fucking me and holding the vibrator to my clit. I am about to go insane.

Then he pulls the plug out of me and before I can understand what is happening he pushes his hard, big cock into my pre-stretched hole.

Oh wow. He puts the vibrator aside again and now holds me with both hands on my hip. His pushes are very slow and gentle at first, but then he gets faster and faster.

I feel how my body reacts to it. Goosebumps form on my arms and I get very hot. Again I hear the buzzing, but this time he grabs my hand and pushes the vibrator in. I hold it against the clitoris myself, close my eyes, enjoy his hard, powerful thrusts and then I come again. Only shortly before he also almost comes. He pulls his cock out, turns me on my back, looks me in the eyes and then shoots his complete load from below over my entire body. My pussy, my belly, my tits and even my face are now properly deliciously covered. This makes me so horny that I could come right back.

I take my vibrator again, squeeze the last drop from his still hard cock and come right back while I rub his cock and rub his sperm on my breasts.

Exhausted, I let myself fall onto my bed while he withdraws and quickly disappears into the bathroom. I look for my bathrobe and wait for him to come back.

I want to say something, but he silently puts his finger on my mouth and then gets dressed.

Wordlessly he says goodbye to me with a smile and a kiss on the cheek and then he is gone.

Wow... I would never have dreamed that my evening would turn out to be quite so exciting after all.

A special massage

It's one of those days again. One of those days where everything just goes wrong. First of all, my best friend cancels on me for the weekend, which I happened to be really looking forward to. Then, I get all the trouble at work for a project that has been completely run into the wall, and for which I am, ok, partly responsible. And then I come home and find that my kitchen is underwater because some pipe in the basement is clogged and now everything is pushed up through my sink.

Annoyed, I start mopping the floor, and then sit down on the sofa with a huge glass of wine. I'm excited for the last episode of a series I've been hooked on that I saved especially for tonight, but of course in line with this day going so horribly, the internet doesn't work properly and I can't finish it.

It feels like the final straw and I'm about to cry, but then I pull myself together and take a deep breath. Everything will be fine.

I look at my cell phone and see that I have a message. Surprisingly not from my best friend who wants to apologise again for this last-minute cancellation or from my work colleague who left me totally alone in the meeting today, but from Jonas.

I got to know Jonas almost a year ago, when my ex-boyfriend suddenly broke up with me and I fell out of the clouds.

On that first evening when I felt like my life had fallen apart, I went out to partly console myself and partly celebrate a new chapter with my girlfriends and then met Jonas.

He was a very good distraction during that time, and I was all good and ready to jump into a new relationship, but I stopped myself when I took a moment to realise I'm 33 and didn't actually know if that's what I wanted again.

I had been with my ex-boyfriend since junior high, I wanted to start a family with him, build a house and everything. I'd had it all mapped out, the full works.

But it didn't work out and I got the chance to make a new start. Another city, another job, another lifestyle.

I had never been alone before. I didn't know what it was like to go on vacation alone, to eat alone or to go on dates. I had never had a date in my life, so it was one of those classics. My girlfriends would always talk about meeting total strangers from the internet and then having sex with them or not, but I didn't know this at all. My ex-boyfriend was just there and then I was with him. And actually, with Jonas it was similar too. He took me home with him and somehow I ended up staying for a few days. At that time I was staying with a girlfriend after my ex banned me from the apartment.

And then it went on like that. We met, spent time together and at some point he asked me if we were together now.

But no. I realised, this is not how I imagined my new life.

So we ended the relationship before it even started.

I moved and never heard anything more from him again. Until today.

"Hello, Julia. How are you? I haven't heard from you for a long time and wanted to know what you're up to. I know that you moved to Stuttgart and through a project I also ended up there for a few weeks. Maybe we can have a drink together sometime."

Confused, I look at the message. Is he serious? I actually thought he didn't want to have anything to do with me after I turned him down like that.

But maybe he just forgot that again or wants something specific from me?

38

I am curious and want to know what it could be, so I answer.

"Stupid day. But otherwise good. When will you be in Stuttgart?", I ask him.

"Oh. Stupid day doesn't sound good. Can anything be done about it? I got here last week."

Oha. I thought he was fishing to maybe ask me if he could stay with me. Although... that would be a pretty bold move.

"I have wine and actually wanted to watch the last episode of a series, but the internet isn't working. And I just can't think of anything else to do... Can you?"

"Sure. I also have wine and internet. Wanna come over?"

In astonishment I raise my eyebrows. That as quick! Is he hoping that I will have sex with him?

"And then we just watch the show and nothing else?"

"As you wish. I can give you a massage with my magic hands."

I try to remember his massages. Oh, yeah. Magic Hands will do. They were very magical indeed, I remember feeling brand new when he was finished.

I am very close to accepting. But can I really do it? To jump immediately when he calls me?

Then again... I was the one who dumped him. I'm not getting my hopes up that there should be more to it and a massage sounds like what I really want right now.

"Where do you live?" I ask briefly. If I need more than 30 minutes by train, it's a no. But if it's very close by, I'll consider it.

He writes me his address and it's actually only three streets away. I guess I have no excuse now.

So I accept.

"Wonderful. Wine is already cold. White wine. Medium dry it was, right?"

"Right."

I slowly get up from the sofa and go to my bedroom to look for something to wear. I can't possibly show up to him with my sweatpants on. So I get into the shower again, put on fresh underwear and a fresh t-shirt and then I fish a pair of jeans from the stack.

40

I brush my hair again, powder my face and remove the mascara stains under my eyes. Yes, I'm ready to go!

I quickly slip into my sneakers and start running. Should I maybe tell my best friend? What if Jonas has a nasty revenge plot planned? But why should he? He wants to give me a massage and some company. Nothing more.

So I leave it and stand in front of the house instead.

It's a nice apartment building with four apartments inside. What could happen there?

I press the bell that doesn't have his name on it. It probably belongs to the landlord, who occasionally gives it to workers at short notice.

"Hello, 2nd floor", Jonas calls me through the intercom.

His voice still sounds just the same. Warm and friendly.

I hear the door buzzer, push the heavy entrance door open and then enter. Immediately the light goes on and I walk up the two floors.

Jonas stands barefoot in the door frame and grins at me.

"Hello!", he says in his friendly manner and then spreads his arms.

I look at him. He hasn't changed at all. He still wears his blond hair in the same style, still wears the same glasses and his beard is still the same.

"Hey", I wrap my arms back around him and greet him with the same kindness. I soak up his familiar scent and then accompany him to his apartment.

"Whose apartment is this?", I ask as soon as I see a piece of furniture that doesn't fit in at all.

"The company I'm working for now," he explains.

"Ah, I see." Everything is so clean and modern. The furniture is either white or black. Jonas prefers rather the rustic wood look, but it still seems somehow cosy.

"Would you like something to drink?" he asks me then. I nod and then follow him into the kitchen, where I watch him take a bottle of white wine out of the fridge and open it.

We then go into the living room and settle down on the grey sofa.

"More comfortable than it looks," I say in astonishment and knock demonstratively on the soft upholstery.

Then we get to talking straight away and sharing what we've been up to since we last saw each other all those months ago, how it went between me and him and how we left things.

"I had a very brief but intense relationship shortly after. Actually, it only ended because she had to go abroad," he says and I immediately feel sorry for him. He really has no luck with women.

"And you?" he asks me.

I'm thinking... I moved quite hastily last year. I was able to stay with my girlfriend for a few months, but I didn't want to put her through that any longer. Then I got the job offer in the other city and looked for something else. And then I was so stressed out with the move, the new city and settling in that I didn't really think about dating at all.

"I was rather busy with my new life. You know... I've never been alone before and I had to learn how to do it. And then somehow, here we are today."

"So you haven't had a man since... me?", he asks me astonished.

That is of course not quite true. There were one or two. A spontaneous one night stand after a club night, kissing at a Christmas party and a flirt at a birthday party. But actually, nothing worth mentioning.

We change the subject, talk about his job and Stuttgart. I give him tips on where he can eat well, where he can get a good drink in the evening and where the best place to go running is.

At some point we have emptied the first bottle of wine and become a little more relaxed. Especially me.

"What about that massage you promised me?" I ask quite directly.

"You're welcome to have it now," he tells me and gets up immediately.

"Okay. I also get up from the sofa and look at him expectantly."

"Best we go to the bedroom."

I follow him and see him light a few candles and play soft music in the background to create the right mood. This has always been very important to him, even back then.

Then he clears the blankets from his bed and provides a bottle of massage oil.

"Do you want to take your clothes off?" he asks.

44

Reluctantly I take off my shoes, then my socks and then open my jeans. Then I pull my t-shirt over my head and look at it.

"It will probably be more comfortable if your bra comes off too," he says afterwards.

I open the bra and throw it on the floor with the other things.

Then I quickly turn around and lie down on the bed. I don't know why I'm being so difficult. He already knows me naked anyway. But, it has been a year.

He sits down next to me and then spreads oil on my back, I can tell from the smell that it's the same oil that he always used and it starts coming back to me. I immediately feel comfortable and secure. I close my eyes and enjoy his gentle touches. How he caresses my back, my shoulders and arms. And then moving a little deeper. He rubs my legs with the oil before he turns back to my back, which he now works a little harder. He kneads my neck, my shoulders and my arms. He does the same with my legs.

And then it moves a little higher again. His fingers are now lying on my bottom. I put on a rather tight panty with half of my ass sticking out. He is now working on it without soaking the fabric in oil.

"Would you like to take it off?" he asks me. Without thinking about his words, I grab the panties by the sides and pull them down.

I feel him dripping even more oil on me and rubbing it. But this time he concentrates only on my bottom. Carefully he smears it with it and with every movement he rubs it a little deeper. Until he has reached between my legs. I groan slightly. This soft touch at exactly this point feels so good. And it seems so random. Somehow unintentional. And that makes it even better.

His hands massage my bottom again and then he lets one hand slide between my legs. And then, slowly, gently, he moves his hands over my clitoris again and again. I groan with pleasure.

Oh, how good that feels.

This time he takes a little more time. While one hand is lying on my butt, the other is massaging me between my legs. Again and again he runs his fingertips over my pearl. Over and over again.

I lie totally relaxed on my stomach. My face is now lying on my flat hands and my breath is slowly getting faster.

My abdomen tenses up all by itself as he continues to rub his fingers over my clitoris.

46

I am so relaxed that I would easily reach climax and I'm pretty sure he knows that.

He continues, spreads some more oil on me and then I feel a finger slowly penetrating me. He now massages me from the inside. He still knows exactly how I like it best and implements this perfectly. One finger is deep inside of me, while he still touches my clitoris with the other finger very lightly.

Then he suddenly withdraws again. I feel his hands on my back again, which he massages and strokes. The tension from my abdomen disappears again and I calm down a little bit. Nevertheless I want him to continue with it, so I let him. I enjoy it as it builds and builds. He will certainly not let me go unsatisfied.

Again his hands wander deeper. Over my bottom, my thighs and then my calves, which he massages vigorously. Then he goes a little higher again. His hands are now working my thighs and whenever he raises them all the way up, I feel his fingers very briefly in my crotch. Oh man. These accidental touches turn me on so much. Of course I know that they are intentional, but they seem so... light and carefree.

I enjoy the way he gently touches my skin and also grips it more firmly when he wants to massage a special area.

I can feel myself switching off again. How I relax and become calmer.

Suddenly he whispers to me to turn around.

I keep my eyes closed and turn on my back.

I feel his hands again on my arms, on my shoulders and then on my stomach. He skips my step for a moment before he turns his attention to my legs again.

And then his hands go up my thighs and I feel him pushing my legs apart a little. I hear something rustling and notice that he has changed his sitting position. He now kneels between my legs, which he now bends and puts my feet on the bed. Wide open I now lie in front of him and let him do it. I trust him completely right now.

Again I feel his hand between my legs. Gently he glides up and down, spreading the oil in my pussy and then he spreads my lips with one hand while the other hand is playing around my clitoris.

Again I groan. Oh man, that feels good. He massages my pearl again and again, moistens it in between so that it is not overexcited and almost drives me out of my mind. But just before I come, he presses two fingers in my pussy.

Oh wow. I didn't expect that just now, but it feels so good the way it fills me up.

He moves his fingers a little back and forth while continuing to tease my clitoris.

He never stops. Again and again he moves over it with his fingertips until I finally come.

It's a very special, deep, relaxed orgasm. One that makes you forget everything around you. One in which all the stress really falls away from you and you lie on the bed completely satisfied and don't want to open your eyes anymore because you are afraid that the pleasant feeling will then disappear immediately.

Jonas slowly withdraws from me. He carefully drives over my legs and over my arms. He lets me enjoy my climax before he brings me back to reality.

"How do you feel?" he asks me.

"Totally relaxed," I answer honestly.

"I'm glad."

He gives me a towel so I can get rid of the oil and afterwards he even silently watches the last episode of my favorite show with me, even though he has already seen it.

Considering the day I've had, I couldn't even have dreamed it would end with me feeling so very deeply relaxed.

Turning 30 in a hostel in Barcelona

It's a big time - my thirtieth birthday! Phew ... 30. Saying goodbye to my twenties! Ten years ago I often imagined this time. In my imagination I'd have a secure job, would be married and already have a child. The second baby would be on the way and my husband and I would be in the middle of renovating our house, somewhere on the outskirts of town, with a big garden and two floors.

The reality, however, looks quite different. I barely keep my head above water with odd jobs, I live in a tiny one-room apartment and I don't even a boyfriend, let alone a husband.

What I do have is numerous other single friends, who take part in any spontaneous antics with me, so there's that!

And so, speaking of spontaneous antics, it happens that I am sitting on a plane right now on my way to Barcelona. I mean, even if my life isn't going according to 'plan', at least my party will be great. And which place would be more suitable to ring in my thirtieth year than Barcelona?

My friends are not that short of money and suggested that I come along to stay with them in a chic hotel right in the center. But I didn't exactly want that. I don't want to admit to myself that I'm already turning 30 and now I only stay in nice, quiet and clean hotels. Then I would feel old!

For me, a simple loft bed in a hostel is enough and so I convinced them that as we'd save so much money on the overnight hotel, they'd have more to spend on something else. I mean, I'd much rather have a chic, new leather bag or new shoes instead of a stay in a hotel.

They weren't exactly enthusiastic, but as it's my birthday, I got my way!

"Wow. Sophie, are you really serious?" my friends ask me as the cab driver throws us out in front of the hostel.

The facade of the building is colorfully painted and directly in front of the entrance are several tables and benches on which numerous young people sit. They are 18 or 19 at most.

"Oh, come on. It won't be that bad and it's sure to be funny if nothing else.," I say and dig the reservation out of my pocket. I walk straight through the entrance and towards the employee with the many piercings and colorful hair.

"Hola!", I say cheerfully and hand him the printed note. He checks us in and then hands us five keys. One for each.

"Where are we going?" Klara, my best friend, wants to know.

I show us the way and only five minutes later we're standing panting on the third floor. I hold my card against the door lock and watch how the little lamp turns green. The door opens and we enter.

"Seriously?!" John, another good friend of mine, asks, exasperated.

We are standing in a somewhat cramped room with three bunk beds. The floor is made of cheap linoleum, orange curtains hang from the windows and in the corner there is a small sink with a mirror. Six lockers are on the other side. However, you had to bring your own lock, which of course none of us thought of.

"I'm sleeping in the bottom bunk," I say quickly and secure the first bed.

My friends spread out over the remaining beds and we stare at the last empty bed.

"Does this stay free?" Karla asks.

I shrug my shoulders. I only booked five beds and there was no five-bed room. So we were probably put into a six-bed room.

"Hopefully someone won't come here in the middle of the night and turn on the light," says John annoyed. "And where is the bathroom?"

He searches the walls for another door that could lead to the bathroom, but finds nothing.

"In the corridor", I say sheepishly and feel the annoyed looks of the others.

"You didn't even want to pay the 10 Euro surcharge for your own bathroom?!"

"10 Euro per night! That's a lot", I defend myself. I'm sure you can get lunch and dinner with that.

We all get changed, go to the bathroom one after the other and then explore the city. Some of my friends have already been here and show us around. It is really super nice here. Everything is so colorful, so loud, so busy.

In the evening we choose a nice restaurant, eat paella and drink lots of beer.

Afterwards we stagger happily back to our hostel room and realize that we are no longer alone. Someone is already asleep in the bed above me.

"I think this is a guy," whispers John. I can't quite make it out. His blonde hair goes down to his chin and he has laid his face against the wall. It could also be a girl with short hair. His clothes may suggest male, but maybe it's one of those super sporty active backpackers who are more into functional clothing than flowery numbers.

We try to find our things together as quietly as possible and then we go to the bathroom.

"When do we get up?", I hear Klara whispering.

"Breakfast is served at 7:00," I reply.

"Seven o'clock? That's five hours from now. Until when?"

"Until 9:00."

"In the hotel we would have had breakfast until 11am", I hear an annoyed voice murmuring from the other corner. But then I fall asleep and wake up to the bed shaking in the early hours of the morning.

Confused, I open my eyes and see the new room occupant squatting in front of me and rummaging around in his backpack. He is wearing only boxer shorts. He must have taken off his T-shirt in the night. I watch him with half open eyes. What I see pleases me. I like it a lot. He is probably a good bit younger than me. Maybe 19 or 20. His blond hair falls into his forehead and he keeps trying to pinch it behind his ears with his fingers. He seems to be looking for something and pulls one garment after the other out of his huge suitcase.

I look at his upper body. He is quite well trained, has a good chest and arm muscles. Maybe I can even see a six-pack there. But it's a bit too dark for that.

Suddenly he looks at me. He has noticed that he is being watched. His blue eyes shine and he grins at me. Then he nods.

"Morning," he says with an accent I've never heard before. Probably a native speaker, but it doesn't sound like American or British English.

South African? New Zealander? I stare at his backpack again. His passport has fallen out of the front pocket and I see that he is from Australia.

Phew... an Australian surfer boy. Hot.

He has found what he was looking for and then disappears.

"Who's making noise this early?" I hear someone mumbling.

"No-one. Go back to sleep," I reply and turn around once more. There are still two hours until 9 o'clock. We should really use them to sleep.

Totally overtired, we stand in the half-empty dining room at 8.30 am and look at the buffet. Cornflakes, toast, rolls, jam and cheese are ready.

"No eggs?" Karla asks disappointedly.

"At 4€ per breakfast? What do you think?" John replies and starts loading his plate with toast and cheese.

I pour myself a cup of coffee and mix myself a muesli. There is an abundant fruit basket and I don't know what the others have. This is more choice than I usually have in the fridge at home.

We stay seated until 9 am and then we're sent outside by a member of the hostel staff because they want to clean up.

"And now?", asks Sonja, another member of the group.

"The weather is great. Let's go to the beach!", I suggest. Tomorrow is my birthday and we've already planned that we absolutely have to celebrate there. Until then, I don't want to go on a strenuous city tour, so as to avoid being too exhausted in the evening. So lazing around in the sun would be just perfect.

The others feel the same and a little later we are lying on the deserted city beach.

We enjoy the sun, the cooling in the sea and one cold beer after another, which we buy from the beach vendors.

At some point I see a blond man with a surfboard running into the sea. He looks quite familiar to me.

"That's the guy from our room!" I say then and point to him.

"Ooh, nice!" Karla calls and we watch him jump on his board, paddle and then ride a wave. Oh yes. He's definitely very nice to look at.

The midday sun comes and we look for a nice beach restaurant before we go back to our towels to enjoy the last rays of sunshine. At some point I nod off and when I wake up I hear that Australian accent again. I turn around and see that the guy from our room is sitting next to John and Karla, excitedly explaining something to them.

"Oh hey!" he says when he realises I'm awake.

"Just trying to explain surfin' to ya mates", he explains and I see his surfboard lying next to him.

I join them, get another round of beer and in the course of the afternoon I learn a lot about our room neighbor. His name is Daryl, he's 20 and is currently traveling through Europe before he wants to start his studies in Sydney. He wants to become a marine biologist and do something against coral death.

He's funny, entertaining and totally open. So I decide without further ado that he should definitely come along when we celebrate my birthday later on. Of course he agrees immediately.

We hurry back to the hostel, change our clothes and then look for a nice bodega to eat at and drink the first litres of sangria.

And then we move on to the fullest club we can find.

I love it when everyone huddles closely together and then goes off together to the music.

The evening is a lot of fun, and just before midnight we all gather on the street and make a toast: to me and my birthday.

Then somehow everything happens very quickly. I lose my group on the way back to the club. I headed for the toilet for the twentieth time, and when I came back, there was no one left. I searched everything. I went to the bar, to the dance floor, even to the smoking area, but they were no longer there.

Until suddenly someone tapped me on the shoulder. I turned around and stared into the blue eyes of Daryl.

"Oh, thank God!", I scream and fall around his neck overjoyed.

I mean, being alone in a club is okay. You can dance, drink and meet new people. But on your own birthday it's pretty sad. That's why I was so happy when Daryl stood opposite me.

He took my hand and led me onto the dance floor. I thought that my friends might be waiting for me there, but even he hadn't seen them for a while. So we danced as a couple. For hours. The music was so terrific, the atmosphere so great. At some point my feet started to hurt and I wanted to sit down for a while. Daryl came along and then one thing led to another and we kissed.

And what a kiss it was. The madness.

"Let's go?!" he now shouts in my ear. I ask him where to go, and he says that he would like to go back to the hostel. He really wants to get up early tomorrow to go surfing.

My feet won't carry me far anyway, so I agree. Hand in hand we walk back to our hostel and stop at almost every corner of the house to make out. Sometimes very gently, sometimes a bit wilder and more passionately and then so hot that I almost took my panties off myself there and then.

But then a few people came by and we moved on, giggling.

When we get back to the room, the light is off and I see that my friends are already lying in their beds and sleeping.

"Uh," Daryl murmurs, and kisses me again.

I'm going back. Is he planning to fuck me here in the room while my friends are also present and sleeping?

He presses me on my bed and continues kissing me.

I clear my throat and point to the others. Without further ado he takes a towel from his bed and throws it over the bar that runs along the upper bed. Then he closes the towel like a curtain so that the others cannot see what is going on in my bed. How clever!

However, he didn't consider that I can get quite loud if I like something well. And somehow he seems to be very quick to know exactly what I like and what I don't.

He pulls my panties off my hips and spreads my legs.

Elegantly he kneels in between them and starts to lick me.

Mhh... his tongue wanders over my clitoris, through my opening to my wet hole and licks me like a young god. It is unbelievable!

I groan, sigh, and let myself fall completely, until suddenly I feel his hand on my mouth.

"Psst!", he goes and brings me back down to earth. I'm still in this cursed hostel room and I can hear comforters rustling because one of my friends is turning around.

I try to be quieter. Close my eyes again and enjoy his tongue on my pussy. He now uses his fingers to penetrate me. First one, then two and then he starts to fuck me with it while his tongue is still on my clit.

Oh, man. I really need to pull myself together right now so that I don't come out loud. He goes on, licks me, fucks me with his fingers and then I just can't hold it back anymore. I come. And I'm coming hard.

I cover my mouth with my hands and try to suppress my moaning, which I halfway succeed in doing, because I do not hear the rustling of the others.

He pauses briefly, lets me enjoy my orgasm and let it fade away.

Then he withdraws and lies down next to me. His hand reaches for mine and guides it to his step. Places it against his cock. His pretty hard and horny cock.

I massage him through his pants and then pull them off him.. Now I have his heavy, thick beating in my hand and I slide up and down it.

I want more. Want to feel this huge cock inside me. First in my mouth, then in my pussy. So I straighten up carefully and get down on my knees to bend down to it.

His tail is now right in front of my face. I first touch it with my tongue, lick it around before I pick it up in my mouth.

As expected, it feels tremendous. I suck on him, suck and hear him moan softly and breathe more intensely.

This time I admonish him to be a little quieter and ask myself how I can ride him best without making too loud noises. The bed already squeaks with every movement.

I turn around and then swing one leg over his legs.

I hold on to his tail and then sit on him.

I feel its tip at my entrance and then slowly lower myself onto it. He penetrates deeper and deeper into me and now I can't help but sigh softly. He feels so good inside me.

I let him slide completely into me and then feel his hands on my hips. He sets the pace. Very slowly I move up and down. Always making sure that the bed doesn't squeak too loudly.

He whispers something. Says something about an idea and then pushes me off.

He pulls his pants up halfway again and then pulls me down from the bed with him. Then he goes to the door and opens it carefully while he continues to hold my hand.

We're now standing in the corridor and he looks around. There is nobody to be seen. He pulls me into the next toilet with him and closes the door behind him.

He presses me with his face to his hand, bends my upper body down and pushes my dress back up.

Then he unpacks his cock and presses it again deep into my pussy.

Oh, God, that feels good.

He starts to fuck me. With deep, long strokes before he gets faster and faster.

Finally I don't have to pay attention to the volume and I groan out my lust.

He claws his fingers into my hips and now he fucks me a little harder.

Until I come another time.

I put my head on my arms and enjoy how my pussy nestles tightly around his cock and I now perceive each thrust even more intensely.

He too is just about ready. He continues, he pushes harder and deeper and then he comes. He comes deeply inside me and I feel a warmth penetrating me. His sperm also fills me completely.

He presses himself firmly against my upper body. I feel his heart beating fast and strong before he withdraws and slowly slides out of me.

He turns me around, kisses me once more, before he pulls his pants up again and opens the door.

"Psst", he says and points to the locked cubicle in the toilet block.

I didn't even realise that we had a listener, but I don't care now.

Silently we sneak back to our room and then sleep in our own beds so that the others don't notice anything the next morning.

But when I sit across the breakfast table without Daryl and they all stare at me with a grin on their faces, I know for sure that despite our best efforts, they heard everything.

Fortunately, no-one says a word...

The Yoga Weekend

I've been looking forward to this moment for a long time. It's been weeks since I had a day off and I have finally made it out of the big city. I can't even remember what a vacation feels like these days. That's why I accepted immediately when my friend Ann invited me to a yoga weekend. Somewhere near the North Sea, in a deep forest, the next stores and restaurants far, far away. Just her, the yoga group and nature.

Yes! Just what I need.

"I'm so looking forward to the weekend," I say, as Anne stands with her car in front of my house.

"At last, no construction site noise to wake me up in the morning. No car horns that startle me in the middle of the night. Only the sound of the sea, the chirping of birds and the calm sounds of music during the yoga classes. Great," I continue, while Anne helps me carry my luggage to the car.

"Yeah. I'm so pleased you said yes on such short notice. None of my friends wanted to come - they get too 'bored' with all the yoga and quiet time.

"All the better for me," I say with a grin as I drop into the passenger seat and fasten my seat belt.

I haven't known Anne for very long. I met her during a yoga class a few months ago and we discovered we live pretty nearby. We often met by chance on the way to the yoga studio and chatted, then we headed home together one evening and got along really well so we arranged to meet for coffee and started doing yoga together in the park and some dinners. She has become a really good friend to me, especially as I'm new to the city!

So I was really pleased of course, when she asked me if I would like to accompany her on the weekend away.

After almost a year in my new job, I've managed to win the liking of my colleagues through my dedication and commitment and work ethic, but it means I haven't yet been able to allow myself a completely free weekend to relax!

With a 4 hour car journey to sit through, Anne turns up the music and we sing along with old songs from the 90s. I can already feel how all the stress from the last months is falling away from me as we drive deeper into the forest and closer to tour home for the weekend.

"Here we are", she says at some point and I look at the little house in wonder. The time seemed to fly by! It never occurred to me that we'd been sitting in the car for several hours.

I get out of the car and see how a small path leads directly to the sandy beach, and utter with delight!

I look around the place - it's a pretty intimate setting, with only room for 20 guests in the house. Everyone arrives on the same day and leaves on the same day, which is nice because you only have to spend the first evening getting to know new faces!

We head into our rooms, which are only equipped with a cosy double bed and a closet. Basic but very welcoming! The balcony has a view out over the sea, and I step outside and take a moment to breathe it all in!

"No distractions," says Anne as she stows her suitcase in the closet.

Once we've unpacked and settled into our room, we head out to the welcome event, where we get to know the other guests and the yoga teachers and hear more about the weekend activities.

The schedule is looking pretty packed. Every morning the first yoga class starts at 6 am. It takes place on the large terrace, so that you can enjoy the first rays of sunshine directly.

Then it's breakfast, then yoga again, a seminar and then lunch.

Then we have some free time before another yoga lesson just before dinner and then we have another seminar before we can go to sleep or enjoy our time in the big living room or on the terrace.

"Quite a full plan, isn't it?", I ask Anne, who has diligently taken notes.

"Yes, but actually you still have a lot of free time in between. You can even book additional yoga classes or use the wellness area or ask for a massage," she explains.

I nod and then follow her back to our room. The first yoga class is about to start and we want to change our clothes.

We arrive in front of the course room, which is still closed. I look around to see the other guests. In the final year of my 20's, I clearly belong to the younger generation. Many of the guests are in their mid, late 30s or in their 40s. Most of them are female, but there are also a few male guests who came with their partners.

"Hello and welcome", the yoga teacher greets us and then leads us into the big, empty room. Huge windows have been installed, which reach from the floor to the ceiling and allow a great view of the dense pine forest.

She introduces us a little, gives us a short overview of the weekend and tells us about the guest teachers who will mainly lead the evening classes.

And then it finally starts.

I enjoy the silence, the gentle but exhausting movements and feel great when the lesson is over.

Anne leaves because she booked a massage and I stay behind with Marta, the yoga teacher. I still have a few questions, mainly because I really want to work more on my flexibility this weekend and I hope she can give me some tips.

"Our guest teacher Patrick is a specialist in this. You are welcome to ask him", she tells me and then points to a small room.

"I think I just saw him go in there."

I nod and then go in search of him.

When I open the door, I end up in a kind of break room for the yoga teachers. About five people are sitting on the sofas, drinking tea and looking at me as I burst in unannounced.

"Oh hello. I was told that I could find a certain Patrick here," I say a little insecurely.

A man with long brown hair, which he has tied into a high bun, stands up and smiles at me.

"I'm that certain Patrick," he says and approaches me.

I look at him. He's tall and slim, looks sporty, but without many muscles. I can well imagine that he is a specialist for flexibility from the way he looks.

His light blue eyes sparkle as he smiles at me and waits for my answer to his question, which I somehow missed.

"How can I help you?" he repeats again.

"Marta told me that you're good at flexibility."

"Yes, she's right. Do you want to improve in that area?" he leads me outside and we end up back in the big yoga room, which is empty now.

"Yes. I often feel very stiff. Especially when I haven't done anything for a long time or when I've been sitting at my desk all day. I'd love to have some exercises for in between and also some I can do regularly to see long-term success," I explain to him.

"I can help you there... what was your name again?", he asks me, without taking his eyes off me.

"Nicole. Nici. You can call me Nici," I say immediately.

"I have to go to a meeting right now, but if you want you can come back in half an hour, Nici. I'll show you some exercises."

I go through the plan in my head, but I can't remember that something is immediately following. So I say yes.

"Wonderful. See you in a minute."

He smiles at me once more and then disappears again into the small room with the other teachers.

I go outside, find a chair with a view of the beach and enjoy the silence and the sound of the sea. It is really peaceful here, so I close my eyes and probably nod off for a moment. I am woken by a gentle push and open my eyes in shock.

"Hey, oh, sorry. I didn't mean to scare you," I hear Patrick say, who is now standing in front of me.

"No problem. I must have dozed off for a minute."

"Yeah, happens fast here. It's all very relaxing I know," he says with a grin.

I slowly stand up again and notice that my neck is stiff. That's what happens when you fall asleep on such an uncomfortable wooden chair.

"Oh dear. That really didn't look comfortable either," he remarks as I turn my neck in all possible directions in front of him.

"Shall I?", he asks and puts his hands on my shoulder.

"Gladly."

He starts to massage me. His hands are heavenly and after only a few minutes I feel much better.

"Thank you," I say and notice nothing more of the tension.

We go into the empty room with only a few yoga mats on the side and Patrick shows me some exercises to become more flexible in general.

He gives me assistance and explains how often I should do it.

After that I ask for more demanding exercises, which probably take me a little longer to do really cleanly, but in the end bring the most benefit.

Patiently he shows me these, until the hall slowly fills up, because the next class is coming.

"Oh...I didn't mean to waste your time. I thought it would only take 20 minutes or so," I finally say when I realize that two hours have already passed.

"No problem. That's what I'm here for. Feel free to ask me again anytime."

I join Anne and the others and at the end of the day I feel really exhausted as I sit in the dining room poking around in my healthy salad.

So I skip the last events, grab a book and a blanket and sit down on the beach.

I really enjoy the silence and solitude very much, I get a few pages further in my book until I suddenly hear footsteps in the sand behind me.

Curious, I turn around and see Patrick, who probably had the same plan as me. He is also standing on the beach with a book and a blanket and wants to find a quiet place.

"Oh, you probably had the same idea," he says with a grin, as he sees me wrapped in the blanket with the book.

"I simply couldn't resist," I say. "Besides, after all those exercises today, I was too tired to attend the seminars."

"Sure ... I understand. May I sit with you or do you want to be left alone?"

I shake my head and put my book aside.

"Unfortunately, the book is not as exciting as we thought. Sit with me quietly."

He lets himself fall into the sand next to me and then we start talking. I find out what he usually does. He finds out what I do and what parts of Germany we actually come from.

"Oh, just the other corner," I notice when he tells me where he lives.

It gets later and later and darker. The sun is almost gone and in front of us the sky and the sea turns pink and orange.

"I love the sunsets here," he enthuses, and then silently watches the sun as it slowly disappears on the horizon.

It's an absolutely perfect moment that I don't want to ruin with any stupid words, so we just sit silently next to each other.

Now that the sun is gone, it's getting a bit colder and I put the blanket a bit tighter around my body. Patrick notices that I am slowly getting cold and without further ado spreads out his arms and blanket and puts it around me as well. We are now sitting very close together. I can feel his warmth and smell his scent. Neither of us says a word.

Then I notice how he turns his face to me and looks at me. I also look at him and see that he is smiling. He comes closer. His face and lips are now right in front of mine and then he kisses me.

Very gently and carefully, but when he notices that I'm not averse, he gets a little stormier. With both hands he now holds my face and searches for mine with his tongue.

We kiss and I forget everything that happens around us. It's getting darker and darker and from the hotel you probably can't see us anymore, which is probably why he becomes a little more courageous. He bites my lower lip and ends the kiss. But only to pull the blanket off my body and to get his hands under my clothes.

I feel his fingertips on my skin and how they move under my T-shirt. I wear a tight sports bra and over it a loose-fitting t-shirt and tight leggings, so it's not so easy for him.

"Shall we go to my room?" he asks.

I nod immediately and think of Anne, who is probably already sleeping in our room. Hopefully he doesn't have a room-mate.

We sneak into the hotel and find ourselves in the lower part of the living area. This is where the teachers and guest teachers will be accommodated.

He unlocks the door and then we stand in a small single room with only a narrow bed.

As soon as the door closes behind us, he starts kissing me again and undressing me. I do it to him immediately and only a few minutes later we are lying naked on his narrow bed.

His hands keep wandering over my body, caressing my arms, my legs and my breasts.

Then he pushes his hand between my legs and touches my clitoris very carefully. But even this gentle touch makes me shudder in delight.

He circles my pearl with his fingertips, taps it again and again and then pulls his fingers over my labia again before he penetrates me with it. I groan loudly. This mixture of gentle and demanding makes me totally wild.

Suddenly he lets go of me and gets up. He pulls me towards him by my legs so that I lean with my back against the wall, then he spreads my legs and gets down on his knees in front of me.

He lowers his head, grabs my thighs and pushes them far apart. I lie completely open now in front of him and watch how he comes closer and closer to my pussy with his face and then starts to lick it. Very gently and carefully, but then more and more passionately and wild. My eyes are now closed and I totally let myself enjoy what he does with me. It feels incredibly good.

Then I feel how he penetrates me with a finger and massages me from the inside. I claw my hand into the blanket. Oh my God. Just what I need now. He pushes another finger into me and continues. With his tongue and his fingers. And then I come. Loud, fierce and exuberant.

I can feel all tension falling away from me and sink into myself as the orgasm is over and it slowly recedes.

I open my eyes and see that he now stands before me. He pulls me to him by the hand and I'm now sitting exactly at the same level as his tail, which is sticking up directly in front of me. It is long and full, and with pleasure I put my hand around it and start to massage it carefully. I move my hand up and down until I come closer with my face. With my tongue I lick over his glans, taste his juice before I slowly take it in my mouth, licking and tasting at first, and then all the way.

I hear his pleasant moaning and feel his hands on my head and his fingers clawing into my hair.

I'm getting faster, and keep working on his tip with my tongue after I push his penis out of my mouth and then push it deep into my throat again.

His breathing becomes faster. He is coming. But just before he's ready, he pushes me away from him and pulls me up. He turns me around, pushes my upper body down so that I can support myself with my knees on the bed and then grabs my hip.

I feel his tail moving through my pussy and groan loudly as he finally pushes it into me.

Mhh... he is big and hard. This time he doesn't start slowly and gently, but fucks me directly with hard, deep thrusts.

I hold on to the bed with my hands and enjoy how he takes me hard and fast from behind.

I hear his moaning, the clapping of skin to skin and then I only feel a twitch. He has come. Into me. But he does not stop fucking me. First slowly, then he gets faster again. His cock is not quite as hard anymore, but I feel him rearing up inside me again.

He turns me over and I lie on my back. He pulls me towards him by my legs and pushes his penis back into my pussy. He turns me on extremely. Now he fucks me again and holds on to my legs again and again - he pushes me with a powerful pulse and pulls on my nipples from time to time. I am just about to come again.

Then he stops.

He moves his penis very gently, but in such a way that my climax is delayed. He puts a finger in my mouth and I suck on it immediately as he moans loudly. Then he continues. He really fucks me again before I come, moaning loudly, and everything contracts inside me. He comes shortly after me and empties himself into me a second time.

He pauses briefly, caressing my body with his hands before he lies down next to me to kiss me.

We grin at each other, then squeeze into the shower as a couple and then fall asleep in his little bed.

Only when the first sunrays shine through the window onto the bed do I wake up again.

"Good morning", I hear him say.

"Good morning", I reply before I get up carefully, give him a smile and then sneak back to my room.

"Where have you been?" Anne asks me in surprise.

"I have worked on my flexibility," I say with a grin.

"I see..."

I quickly change my clothes and hurry with Anne to the terrace where the first yoga class takes place. Patrick is also there, who looks at me with a grin and whispers that he can't wait for the next private lesson...

Made in the USA
Las Vegas, NV
11 October 2023

78929138R00049